The Honey-Guide Bird

Two Traditional Tales from Africa

Contents

Written by Deborah Bawden

Illustrated by Monica Auriemma

The Honey-Guide Bird

"Grandma, Temba won't let me play with him,"
sobbed Kuda. Tears rolled down and streaked through
the dust on his face. "He says I'm too small."

"Oh, the silly boy," Grandma said in a soothing voice.
"Hasn't your brother heard of the clever
honey-guide bird?"

Kuda looked up at his grandma. He always knew when
a story was on its way. Grandma was the best storyteller
and she was very old and very wise. There was nothing
she didn't know.

"The honey-guide bird is very small, the size of this banana," she rumbled, peeling the banana's bright yellow skin for Kuda, "and he doesn't weigh very much, but he manages to fool many creatures bigger than him."

Kuda leant forward excitedly. "How?"

"Well, one day a honey-guide bird defeated a mighty hunter and taught him a lesson he'd never forget. Wild honey is very hard to find, but the honey-guide birds are very clever. They can find wild beehives, but they need help to get the honeycomb out from the hives. So they lead hunters to the hive in return for some of the honeycomb.

One fine, hot day, when the heat was dancing on the ground, a honey-guide bird attracted the hunter Shaka's attention. "Chitik-chitik-chitik," he called.

Now Shaka was a greedy man and very selfish, so he quickly grabbed his spear and crept away from his village. He followed the honey-guide bird, thinking all the time of the sweet honey. After following the bird for some time, they reached the bottom of a fig tree.

Shaka collected wood and started a small fire at the bottom of the tree. Then he got a large, dry stick and put it into the fire. As soon as he saw smoke on the end of the stick, he put the cool end in his mouth and started to climb the tree.

As he climbed, he heard
the loud buzzing of the bees
in the hive. Then he could
smell the sweet honey in
the air. Oh, how good was
the thought of sweet,
delicious honey!

He poked the smoking stick into
the hive and the bees flew out
like warriors with spears!

Quickly, Shaka stuck his hand into the hive and pulled out the thick honeycomb. He put it into the pouch around his neck and climbed down.

"Chitik-chitik-chitik," called the honey-guide bird, asking for his reward.

But Shaka walked off into the bush. "Silly little bird. Do you think I'm going to share the honey after I did all the hard work? What can you do – you're so small and *I* am a fierce warrior."

The honey-guide bird never forgot nor forgave Shaka, and he sat and watched him for many months. Then one day, he called out to Shaka again. "Chitik-chitik-chitik."

Shaka grabbed his spear, sure he could fool the bird again.

The honey-guide bird stopped at the base of another fig tree. Shaka couldn't see the beehive, but he trusted the honey-guide bird. Once again, he lit the fire, fetched a stick and climbed the tree.

Imagine his surprise when he got to the place where
he thought the beehive was ... and came face to face
with a sleeping leopard! Luckily, the leopard was caught
by surprise too! It spun around and reached out with
its great, giant paw.

Shaka fell out of the tree into a pile of thorns. When he returned to his village, the doctor removed the thorns, and Shaka learnt never to cross the honey-guide bird, even though it's small.

11

"So you see," said Grandma, "you should never judge someone by their size. Go and tell Temba to let you play!"

As Kuda ran off, Grandma's warm chuckle rumbled from the bottom of her belly like the sound of long-distance thunder rolling over the plains.

Monkey's Heart

In a faraway place, where the land ends and
the Indian Ocean takes over, there's a great wetland.
Under a burning sun and blue, blue sky, lush green plants
and trees grow out of the water as far as the eye can see.
Crocodiles and hippopotamuses swim in the sea,
and then journey through the wetland with
the freshwater fish.

Monkey lived in the wetland. She loved to talk to
the crocodiles because they were ancient creatures
and very wise. Although they were very scary looking
with bumpy skin, hooded eyes and enormous teeth,
if the birds that cleaned the crocodiles' teeth were to
be believed, they were quite harmless, especially after
a good meal.

Monkey also loved to tease the hippopotamuses.
They looked gentle, but they were very grumpy and could
charge really fast through the water when Monkey
swung out of a tree and startled them or managed to
pull their funny little tails.

Of all of Monkey's friends in the wetland, her favourite was Shark. Monkey would sit for hours in her favourite tree at the edge of the turtle beach and chat to him.

Shark had travelled all over the world, and he'd tell her about the beautiful coral reefs and the colourful fish that could be found beneath the ocean.

As she listened to Shark's stories, Monkey felt her life was a little small. She'd never travel across the Indian Ocean, through the North Sea to the Atlantic Ocean. And the more stories Shark told her, the smaller Monkey's life felt.

One evening, Shark told Monkey how he'd chased whales and swum alongside the North Sea trawlermen, devouring any fish they threw back into the sea.

After he'd gone, Monkey leapt back through the trees.
"What's the matter?" twittered the other monkeys.
"You're quieter than normal."

"Oh ..." sighed Monkey. "I've been chatting with my
friend, Shark. He's back from one of his great adventures.
I wish I could travel as far and as fast as he does and not
just be stuck on the edge of the wetland."

"What have we told you about sharks and their stories?"
the other monkeys said. "Don't trust that big grin
of his and those grand tales. It's fine for him, but not
for you. Everything you need is here where you're safe.
You belong in the trees! Out there is the unknown."

This was exactly what had attracted Monkey to Shark
in the first place! She wanted to travel on Shark's back
to the great unknown and have lots of adventures.

The next day, Monkey met Shark by the edge
of the wetland.

"Hey, what's your favourite food?" Shark asked with
a big toothy smile. "I love sardines. There are lots in
the wetland – that's why I like living here.
Oh, and because I enjoy your company,
as well."

Monkey didn't eat any food she couldn't get in
the wetland, but last summer a swallow had brought
her some palm hearts from Zanzibar. They'd been
delicious and so juicy.

Shark hung on her every word as she described the hearts
and where they'd come from and how delicious they were.
Then, with a wide grin and a flick of his tail, he was off
on another adventure.

It was a long time before Monkey and Shark met
up again. She'd settled back into her colourful life
and watched as the turtles laid their eggs on the beach,
and then as their babies hatched and made their way
to the ocean.

As she sat there watching the turtles bobbing
on the waves, in swished Shark.

"Hello!" he grinned. "I've some exciting news."

"What is it?" Monkey had never seen Shark so happy.

"I've found some palm hearts! Jump on to my back, and I'll take you to them."

Monkey was so excited. An adventure with her best friend to eat her favourite food! Without a backward glance, she leapt out of the tree and on to Shark's back. This is what she'd been dreaming of!

Shark swam very fast, but Monkey felt safe on his back.
Soon the wetland disappeared behind them, but Monkey
didn't care. What a view of the ocean!

Then Shark spoke quite gently: "I was hoping to trade with you – a delicious palm heart for your heart. What do you say?"

Monkey froze with fear. She sat very still and looked at the vast ocean surrounding her. The great unknown. She felt very small, and very far away from the wetland.

"Oh, of course, that seems like such a good trade, but I wish you'd said something before we left land. You see, my heart is so precious that I always leave it at the top of my tree so that it'll be safe."

Shark groaned and his whole body shook with anger.

"I'll tell you what, if you turn around right now and quickly swim back, I can collect my heart and we can trade. You're such a fast swimmer; we'll be there in no time at all."

26

Shark thought about this for a moment before spinning
around and heading back to the wetland. As soon
as they were close enough, Monkey leapt off his
back and into the trees.

Shark opened his wide mouth. "Throw down your heart!" he called.

But Monkey stayed right where she was. "You may have travelled far and had great adventures, but I'm still cleverer than you. I'll never trade my heart, not for all the palm hearts in Zanzibar!"

Shark gnashed his teeth.
He'd been tricked!

Monkey leapt through the trees, back to the other monkeys.
Never again did she want to go on adventures – or ever
completely trust a shark.

Clever creatures

Ideas for reading

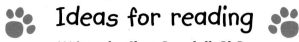

Written by Clare Dowdall, PhD
Lecturer and Primary Literacy Consultant

Reading objectives:
- identify themes and conventions
- discuss their understanding and explain the meaning of words in context
- make predictions from details stated and applied

Spoken language objectives:
- participate in discussions, presentations, performances, role play, improvisations and debates

Curriculum Links: Geography – locational knowledge; Science - Animals

Resources: Materials for mask making

Build a context for reading

- Show children the front cover and read the title. Discuss what kinds of features traditional tales sometimes have.
- Read the blurb to the children. Ask them to think of some clever animal behavior, and explain how this cleverness is used for survival, e.g. being able to change colour.

Understand and apply reading strategies

- Read p2 to the children, emphasising the characters' voices, and reading with expression. Stress that the story should sound like it's being told aloud.
- Ask children to take turns to read p3 aloud to practise reading expressively. Encourage them to help each other and provide positive feedback.
- Focus on developing understanding before reading the rest of the story. Ask children to discuss what the honey-guide bird can do that's clever, and why they lead hunters to wild bee hives. Check that children understand that the hunter and honey-guide bird depend on each other.